Margaret Tempest.

Squirrel Goes Skating was first published
in Great Britain by William Collins Sons & Co 1934

This edition published by HarperCollins*Publishers* 2001
Abridged text copyright © The Alison Uttley Literary Property Trust 2001
Illustrations copyright © The Estate of Margaret Tempest 2001
Copyright this arrangement © HarperCollins*Publishers* 2001
Additional illustration by Mark Burgess
Little Grey Rabbit ® and the Little Grey Rabbit logo are
trademarks of HarperCollins*Publishers* Limited

1 3 5 7 9 10 8 6 4 2

ISBN: 000 198386-5

The HarperCollins website address is: www.**fire**and**water**.com

Printed and bound in Singapore

SQUIRREL GOES SKATING

ALISON UTTLEY
Pictures by Margaret Tempest

An imprint of HarperCollins*Publishers*

E VERYTHING was frozen. Even the brook
which ran past little Grey Rabbit's house on
the edge of the wood was thick with ice.

Each blade of grass had a white fringe, and on every window of the house were Jack Frost's pictures, trees and ferns and flowers in silver. Little Grey Rabbit stood looking at them with delight, wishing they would always be there, in summer as well as winter.

"Grey Rabbit! Grey Rabbit!" called Hare as he came downstairs in his brown dressing gown. "Put some more wood in the fire. It's bitter cold today." He shivered as a draught blew under the door and ran round his feet.

Grey Rabbit left the window and put a log on the fire. She pulled the table closer and drew up the chairs.

"I believe I've got a chilblain," said Hare in a complaining voice, as he examined his toes. "What can you do for it, Grey Rabbit?"

Grey Rabbit went to the medicine cupboard and looked at the bottles which stood in a row.

There was primrose wine for coughs and colds and dandelion for toothache, and dock leaves for bruises, but nothing for chilblains.

"There isn't anything for chilblains," said Grey Rabbit sadly.

"Ow! Ow!" exclaimed Hare, rubbing his toe. "You don't know how it hurts!"

"Moldy Warp once told me to use snow," said Grey Rabbit. She ran outside and scraped the rime from the grass. Then she rubbed Hare's foot until the chilblain disappeared.

"Grey Rabbit! Grey Rabbit!" called Squirrel,
coming downstairs with a shawl over her
shoulders. "You've let the North Wind in!"

So Grey Rabbit put another log on the fire, and sent away the little wind which had rushed in when she went out.

At last they sat down to breakfast, with hot tea and thick buttered toast, and carrot sausages.

"Milk-o," called a voice, and Hedgehog knocked at the door.

"It's fruz today," said he, as he turned a solid lump of milk out of his can. With his prickles all frost covered, he looked like a spiky snowball.

"Come in and warm yourself, do, Hedgehog," said Grey Rabbit.

He stamped his feet at the door, rubbed them on the mat and tiptoed over to the fire. Squirrel chopped off some of the milk and Grey Rabbit gave a cup of tea to the frozen Hedgehog.

As he sipped from his saucer, blowing at the steam, he talked. "There's skating over Tom Tiddler's Way," said he, "and I've heard that everyone is going."

Hare put down his knife and fork.
"Let's go too," said he.
"Hurrah for skating!"
He gobbled up his
breakfast as fast
as he could.

"There's no hurry, Mr Hare," drawled Hedgehog.
"Ice'll wait. Well, I must be getting on.
Thank ye kindly for the tea."

He tiptoed out again, leaving
a little stream on the floor.

Grey Rabbit wiped it away,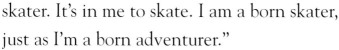
and Hare jumped up from the
table. "Have you ever seen me
skate?" he asked. "I'm a very good
skater. It's in me to skate. I am a born skater,
just as I'm a born adventurer."

"And a born boaster," whispered Squirrel
to the teapot.

"Did you ever hear how I skated round Lily Pond backwards, and passed all the other skaters going forwards?"

"Not now," said Grey Rabbit gently. "We must get our skates cleaned, and the house tidied and pack the lunch."

"And put on our best clothes," added Squirrel.

Hare went out to clean the skates, Squirrel disappeared upstairs, and little Grey Rabbit did everything else as quickly as she could.

She washed the dishes and swept the floor, she made up the fire and chopped the sticks for the next day, she dusted the kitchen and made her bed, she cut the sandwiches and packed them in the basket.

When she stood ready to go, with a little muffler round her neck, she called Hare and Squirrel.

Hare came running in, with a basket full of icicles. "I've been collecting these, to take for drinks," he said excitedly. "You just suck one like this" – and he held one in his mouth – "and it makes a nice watery drink."

"That's splendid," said Grey Rabbit, "but you haven't changed your dressing gown! Are you going to skate in it? And where are the skates?"

"Oh, Jemima!" exclaimed Hare. "I forgot." And he hurried off to get ready.

"Squirrel! Squirrel! Are you ready?" called Grey Rabbit at the foot of the stairs.

"Coming in a moment," said Squirrel, and Grey Rabbit took a last look round. The table was laid ready for their return. There was a herb pie, an apple tart, some jam puffs, and cob-nut cutlets.

"Can you come here?" called Squirrel in a muffled voice. Grey Rabbit and Hare both hurried to Squirrel's room.

A strange sight met their eyes.

A green dress was jumping round and round the room, with two little paws waving wildly in the air. A tail stuck half-out of one of the sleeves, and Squirrel was so hopelessly entangled that her head couldn't find a way out at all.

Hare and Grey Rabbit sank down on the bed helpless with laughter.

When at last they straightened her out they found she had decked herself with little green bows on her ears, and hung a locket around her neck.

"Oh, Squirrel, you cannot go like that!" said little Grey Rabbit.

So Squirrel untied her ear ribbons, but insisted on keeping the ribbon on her tail, and the locket round her neck.

Off they went at last, Grey Rabbit carrying the basket of food, Hare swinging the basket of icicles in one paw and the kettle in the other, and Squirrel following daintily with the skates dangling on her arm.

They locked the door, and put the key on the windowsill. Over it they sprinkled leaves and grass with a few icicles.

"Nobody would guess that was a key," said Hare, and the others agreed.

The world gleamed like a sparkling diamond, and
the air was sweet as spring water. The three
animals ran down the lane and across the fields
towards Tom Tiddler's Way.

Little hurrying footsteps came along a side path, and a party of brown rabbits, each with a pair of skates, joined them.

"Fine day, Squirrel! Fine day, Grey Rabbit! Fine day, Hare!" said they.

Hare led the way, past Moldy Warp's house, through the fields, and under tall bare trees.

"Stop a minute," called a voice as they crossed a frozen stream, and a handsome Water Rat joined them. Grey Rabbit was a great friend of Water Rat's. He often showed her where the best watercress grew.

"It's not often I get the chance of such fine company," said he, smiling at Squirrel. "Are you going to the fair, Miss Squirrel?"

"I'm going skating," answered Squirrel, giving her bows a twitch.

By this time they had reached the pond. Many animals were on the ice, and the air was filled with merry cries and laughter. The newcomers sat down on the bank and put on their skates. Soon they were laughing and shouting with the others as they skimmed over the ice.

Hare tried to do the outside edge, and got mixed up with the skates of a white duck. He fell down with a thump and bruised his forehead. Grey Rabbit ran up and rubbed him with her paw. She dusted the powdered snow off his bright coat, and helped him to his unsteady feet.

Moldy Warp was there, skating as well as he did everything else, slow and sure, avoiding Hare's wild dashes, giving a kindly word here and there.

"I'm hungry," called Hare. "Let's have lunch."

So they joined Mrs Hedgehog, who sat watching young Fuzzypeg.

Grey Rabbit unpacked the basket, and Squirrel invited Water Rat, Moldy Warp, Mrs Hedgehog and Fuzzypeg to join them. There was enough for all. Hare's icicles were very thin by now, but he handed round the basket and each sucked the sweet cold ice.

Soon Grey Rabbit had the kettle boiling and hot drinks of lemonade for everyone.

"Sour! Sour!" grimaced little Fuzzypeg, but his mother nudged him to remember his manners.

They all returned to the ice and skated until the red sun set behind the far hills, and the air took on a new fresh coldness. The sky was violet, and the dark shadows spread across the fields as the animals removed their skates and set off home.

"It *has* been a jolly day," said Grey Rabbit to Water Rat and Moldy Warp. "Goodbye. Perhaps we will come again tomorrow."

"Goodnight. Goodnight," resounded round the pond.

"Did you see me skate?" asked Hare excitedly. "I did the double-outside-edge backwards and a figure seven on one leg."

"I saw all the little rabbits and fieldmice you knocked down," said Squirrel severely.

Grey Rabbit cried, "Hush! Don't make a noise at night. Wise Owl doesn't like it."

So they walked softly along, and the stars came out to keep them company.

The key was on the windowsill, under the pile of grass, but there were footprints in the garden.

"Someone's been here while we've been skating," said Squirrel, looking anxiously around.

They all hurried inside the little house, and stared in dismay at the sight.

On the table lay the remains of the feast, only crusts and dirty dishes.

"Oh! Oh!" cried Hare. "I was so hungry, and there isn't enough for a bumble bee."

"Oh! Oh!" cried Squirrel. "I was so thirsty, and there isn't a drink for a minnow."

"Oh! Oh!" cried Grey Rabbit. "I left such a feast, and now look at the dirty tablecloth and the broken dishes and the spilt wine!"

"Oh! Who's been here since we've been gone?" they said all together, running to the larder.

Not a scrap of food remained! And over the floor were footprints, ugly footprints.

They ran softly up to the bedrooms, each with a little candlestick.

"There's no one in my attic," whispered Grey Rabbit, as she peeped in her room.

"And there's no one in my room," said Hare.

"Oo-Oo-Oo," squeaked Squirrel. "Somebody's sleeping in *my* bed! Oo-Oo-Oo."

They peered through the open door, but all they could see was a long, thin tail hanging down on the floor and long black whiskers sticking out of the sheets.

"Who is it?" whispered Squirrel.

"It's Rat's tail," said Hare.

"They're Rat's whiskers," said Grey Rabbit, below her breath.

"Then it must be Rat himself," sobbed Squirrel.
They looked at the lump under the sheets
and listened to the snores which came from the
comfortable Rat. Then they tiptoed downstairs.

"What shall we do?" they asked each other,
as they stood in the untidy kitchen.

Hare trembled. Squirrel wiped her eyes on
her tail. Grey Rabbit shivered as she thought
of Rat's sharp teeth.

"I'm very good at catching
foxes," said Hare boldly,
"but I don't remember
how to catch a Rat."

"I once caught a Weasel,"
said Grey Rabbit shivering,
"but I couldn't catch a Rat."

"We don't want to catch him," said Squirrel. "He's caught already. We want him to go out of my bed."

The others looked at her in surprise and admiration. "Let's shoo him out," she continued.

"But he ought to be punished," objected Grey Rabbit. "He ought to remember his wickedness."

"When I want to remember anything I tie a knot in my handkerchief," said Hare.

"But I don't think Rat has a handkerchief," said Grey Rabbit.

Then Squirrel spoke these astonishing words, "I can tie knots," said she. "I will tie a knot in Rat's tail, and it will never, never, never come undone. Then he will never, never, never forget his wickedness."

Squirrel crept upstairs again and Hare and Grey Rabbit followed.

She picked up the long tail, and twisted it and turned it, and doubled it, and looped it, till it made one great knot, and Rat never woke for he had eaten and drunk so much.

They shut the door and ran downstairs with beating hearts.

"Now we must frighten him away," said Grey Rabbit.

Hare took the tongs and poker, Grey Rabbit took two saucepan lids, and Squirrel took the bundle of skates. They hammered and banged against the bedroom door, and made such a clang and clatter, such a rattle and racket, such a jingle and jangle, that the Rat awoke.

He sprang out of bed, bewildered, opened the window, and jumped on to the flower bed below.

"Whatever's that a-bumping and a-clumping behind me?" said he to himself, and he turned round to find his tail in a knot.

He ran down the paths with the knot reminding him of his wickedness all the way, and he didn't like it at all.

At last he sat down and tried to undo the knot, but just then Wise Owl came sailing along the sky, over the meadows and woods.

He spied Rat down below, twisting and turning, as he tried to unfasten his tail.

"Hallo, Rat!" said he, and he flew down to look at the unfortunate animal. "Been in mischief?" He chuckled, and then soundlessly rose from the bough and flew away.

In the little house Grey Rabbit put clean sheets on Squirrel's bed, and Squirrel swept the floor, and Hare made a fire in the kitchen to cheer everybody up as there was no food.

Suddenly there came a knock at the door.

Thump! Thump! Thump!

The three animals looked at one another. "Is it Rat come again?" they asked anxiously.

"Grey Rabbit! Open the door," cried a voice.

"That's Mole," said Grey Rabbit happily, and she flung wide the door.

Moldy Warp staggered in with a big hamper, followed by Water Rat with another.

"I thought we would end the skating day with a feast," said Mole.

They both opened the baskets and took out some buttered teacakes, a cranberry jelly, some raspberry jam and dandelion sandwiches and a big plum cake with icing on the top.

"Hurrah!" cried Hare. "Hurrah!" said Squirrel.
"Talluraley!" sang little Grey Rabbit, dancing
round the room.

"Hedgehog is bringing an extra can of milk," said
Moldy Warp. "I thought you might be short.
Somebody whispered that you had a visitor today."

"Squirrel did have company," laughed Hare, "and she tied a bow on his tail!"

After supper they sang songs. They ended with "He's a jolly good fellow," and toasted Mole and Water Rat in a bottle of primrose wine which Rat had overlooked.

"Old friends to meet, old wine to drink, and old wood to burn," said Mole, holding high his glass, and then he and Water Rat said goodbye, and walked along the quiet field paths to their homes.